Pirates Ahoy!

Written by Lisa Thompson
Pictures by Craig Smith

The pirates looked out to sea.

The red pirate called,
"Seagull ahoy!"

"Turtle ahoy!"
called the blue pirate.

The sea dog was called Bones.

He looked out to sea, too.

"Mermaid ahoy!"

The green pirate
was called Lizzie.

"Dolphin ahoy!"

"Look out!"
called the parrot.

"Whale ahoy!"

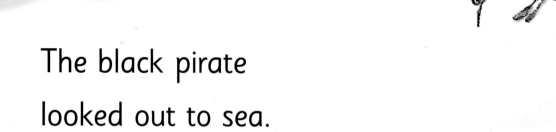

The black pirate
looked out to sea.

"Oh no! Shark ahoy!"

Then the sea monster
looked at the pirate ship.

"Pirates ahoy! Yum!"